Grieser

I'm Glad I'm Your
GRANDPA

written by Bill and Kathy Horlacher
illustrated by Kathryn Hutton

Library of Congress Catalog Card No. 86-63569
©1987. The STANDARD PUBLISHING Company, Cincinnati, Ohio
Division of STANDEX INTERNATIONAL Corporation. Printed in U.S.A.

I'm glad I'm your grandpa!
Please let me say why . . .

I'm glad I'm your grandpa
when you walk by my side—

or we get on our bikes,
and we go for a ride.

I'm glad I'm your grandpa
when our team's doing well—
and because we're excited,
we let out a yell.

I'm glad I'm your grandpa
when we see something old—
or you show lots of interest
when a story is told.

I'm glad I'm your grandpa
when we visit the zoo—
and you laugh at the animals
doing tricks just for you.

I'm glad I'm your grandpa
when you give me your hand—
while we watch a parade
with a big marching band.

I'm glad I'm your grandpa
when you send me some mail—

or you watch me do work
with a hammer and nail.

I'm glad I'm your grandpa
when we study a bug—

or you help me in cleaning
a spot off the rug.

I'm glad I'm your grandpa
when we go out to eat—
and you give me a smile,
and say, "Thanks for the treat."

I'm glad I'm your grandpa
when you ask me to pray—
so we both can thank God
at the end of the day.

But most of all,
I'm glad I'm your grandpa
Just because you're you.

You're God's wonderful gift to me!